THE Puppy AND THE Ring

Adapted by **Mary Tillworth**
Illustrated by **MJ Illustrations**
Cover illustration colored by **Steve Talkowski**

Based on the teleplay "The Puppy and the Ring!" by **Robert Scull** and **Jonny Belt**

A Random House PICTUREBACK® Book

Random House 🏠 New York

© 2014 Viacom International Inc. All rights reserved. Published in the United States by Random House Children's Books, a division of Random House LLC, 1745 Broadway, New York, NY 10019, and in Canada by Random House of Canada Limited, Toronto, Penguin Random House Companies. Pictureback, Random House, and the Random House colophon are registered trademarks of Random House LLC. Nickelodeon, Bubble Guppies, and all related titles, logos, and characters are trademarks of Viacom International Inc.
randomhouse.com/kids
ISBN 978-0-385-38408-7
Printed in the United States of America
10 9 8 7 6 5 4 3 2 1

Long ago in the land of Bubbledom, there lived a Sun King. Every morning he would make the sun rise with the power of his magic ring—the Ring of the Sun.

Everyone agreed that having both day and night was a wonderful thing—everyone but the Night Wizard. He wanted it to be night forever. So he sent his lobster army to the Sun King's realm to steal the Ring of the Sun.

The Night Wizard's army marched through Bubbledom to the
Sun King's castle. They charged into the throne room and zapped the
Sun King and his guards with magic sleeping moonbeams!

After the Sun King fell asleep, the army took the ring and hid it in
a treasure chest. Then they started their long journey back to the
Night Wizard's realm.

As they marched through Bubbledom, the Night Wizard's lobster army came upon Gil and Molly. The Guppies were selling delicious lemon Bubble Slushies. It was a hot day, and the lobster soldiers were very thirsty. Soon everyone was in line to get a cool drink.

While the lobster soldiers were drinking their slushies, Bubble Puppy bumped into the treasure chest. The lid opened, revealing the Ring of the Sun. When Bubble Puppy went to take a closer look, the ring attached itself around his neck!

"Seize the puppy! Seize them all!" cried the lobster general when he saw the ring on Bubble Puppy.

"Run!" shouted Gil. He, Molly, and Bubble Puppy dashed into the forest. The lobster army followed close behind.

Gil, Molly, and Bubble Puppy raced into the woods, and the footsteps of the lobster army faded away. But then Gil and Molly realized they were lost!

Suddenly, the magical Flutterguppies, Deema and Oona, appeared!

Deema and Oona gasped when they saw the Ring of the Sun around Bubble Puppy's neck.

"If the Sun King doesn't have the ring when the sun goes down tonight, the sun will never come up again!" said Oona. The two Flutterguppies decided to take Gil, Molly, and Bubble Puppy to the Sun King's castle to return the ring.

Deema and Oona led the way out of the forest and up an icy mountain. "Behold the realm of the Snow Guppy!" said Oona.

The mountain was covered in snow clumps that looked like animals. Bubble Puppy barked at a bear-shaped one. The snow clump shook—it was a real bear!

"Time to call for help!" said Oona, pulling out her phone. She frantically dialed the Snow Guppy's number.

The bear paused. It reached into its fur and took out a phone. "Hello?" he said. The bear was the Snow Guppy!

The Snow Guppy magically transformed himself into Goby the Snow Guppy. When he heard about Gil and Molly's quest to return the Ring of the Sun, he agreed to help.

"You'll need my help going down the mountain," he said. "Follow me!"

Goby led the Guppies safely down the side of the mountain and into the realm of the Sun King. They hurried along the path to the castle. They only had a few more hours before sunset!

As they got closer to the castle, Bubble Puppy ran ahead. He crossed a bridge and stopped. He saw some of his favorite treats, Bubble Bites, on the ground!

Bubble Puppy followed the trail of Bubble Bites, crunching away happily. He didn't realize that he was being led into a trap.

As the Bubble Guppies ran to help Bubble Puppy, the lobster general cast a magic moonbeam and the bridge began to crumble!

"Bubble Puppy, you've got to get to the Sun King's castle before the sun goes down!" Gil cried.

Bubble Puppy wriggled free and dashed off—just as the rest of the bridge gave way, sending Gil and Molly tumbling!

Gil and Molly fell down, down, down into the realm of the Underguppy. The Underguppy was a mysterious cloaked figure named Nonny. He commanded an army of bats that lived in underground caves.

Nonny showed Gil and Molly the way back to the surface. He also gave them a hoodie of invisibility to help them find Bubble Puppy.

Gil and Molly raced to the Sun King's throne room, where they found
Bubble Puppy locked in a cage and the Night Wizard trying to remove
the ring. Gil used the hoodie of invisibility to try to free Bubble Puppy
while Molly crept up the throne stairs to awaken the Sun King.

Gil opened the cage that held Bubble Puppy. "Run, Bubble Puppy!" he called, slipping off the hoodie of invisibility.

The Night Wizard looked around and spotted Molly. He flew up the stairs and stopped her. "Seize them!" he ordered his guards.

Just then, Oona, Deema, Goby, and Nonny arrived. Oona and Deema turned into Flutterguppy butterfly tornadoes. Goby turned into the ferocious Snow Guppy bear. Nonny brought his army of bats with him. Together they chased away the Night Wizard's army!

Gil saw a tapestry that showed the Sun King making the sun rise by pointing the ring at the sun. That gave him an idea.

Gil held Bubble Puppy up to the setting sun. The ring glowed, and the sun began to rise. It was daytime again! The Sun King woke up with a yawn.

"Nooo! My plan is ruined!" cried the Night Wizard. "Now it will be day again!"

"But daytime is awesome!" said Gil. "You can play outside with your friends!"

The Night Wizard shook his head. "I don't have any friends."

Molly smiled. "We'll be your friends!"

And as the warm sun shone down, everyone went outside to play and drink Bubble Slushies. "What a wonderful day!" cheered the Night Wizard, and he smiled at his new friends. The land of Bubbledom was saved!